we all have CHOICES

A Love Story

Barb Shannon

PublishAmerica
Baltimore

© 2004 by Barb Shannon.

All rights reserved. No part of this book may be reproduced, stored in a retrieval system or transmitted in any form or by any means without the prior written permission of the publishers, except by a reviewer who may quote brief passages in a review to be printed in a newspaper, magazine or journal.

First printing

ISBN: 1-4137-5328-0
PUBLISHED BY PUBLISHAMERICA, LLLP
www.publishamerica.com
Baltimore

Printed in the United States of America

To the man who made it all possible

My heartfelt thanks to my family and friends who have endured my dreaming and supported me as I have made a dream into reality. To my daughters, Chele and Lissa, who taught me, as I taught them, that you can do and be anything in this life. To Becky, my first proof reader, for her thoughts and suggestions. A big thank you to Vicki; I truly would not be at this point if not for her! And, of course, to my publisher, who believed I had something to say and allowed me to say it.

PRELUDE

All of life is a journey –
or rather a series of journeys.
As one goal is reached (or abandoned);
as the particular path we are on seems to end;
as an accomplishment is completed;
we find the journey is not over,
but carrying us into the next phase of life,
as we constantly grow and change.

and so it is with love. .
a journey of two separate hearts.

Who can define love?
For every person in love
the definition is different
(and if you've been in love more than once
your definition of love has more than likely changed).

As two people fall in love and grow
that love changes also;
as two separate hearts try to meld to make a life together
they journey with each other down an unknown path.

this is one journey of love. . . . .

Chapter 1

In bed at night, as I am drifting off to sleep, I find myself still counting the days that I last spoke with him. I don't know what I miss most: him, the island, being in love, not feeling loved now. I only know that I still wish that it had worked. What a glorious love affair it was!

It began as I felt the pull of the islands and knew it was time once more to plan days of rest and relaxation in a place far from home. I came in search of sea and sand and for the sun to warm my soul. And, if the truth be known, I came in search of my island dream; of a man to share my life in the warmth of the sun, the lull of the sea.

When did the phone calls start? All I know is that after spending five days on the island with him, I was smitten. Then the phone calls began and a vacation fling was fast turning into something more.

Always having dreamed of an island life, this man was fulfilling my dreams. It seemed to be just what I was looking for – the whole package. But, I knew to go slowly – I had been here before and was not going to make the same mistake twice.

For now I was content to dream my dream and see where it would lead. Again, I was on a journey, of the heart and mind, with a man two thousand miles away. I figured I had nothing to lose as I had no romance going at home. I was willing to see where this could all take me.

Soon, we were speaking every night and making plans to see each other again over the Christmas/New Year holidays. Til then I write of my feelings, my doubts, my concerns; little knowing the choices I would have to make in the future . . .

Island time
Slow your pace
Let your mind run free

Look at the moon
See the stars
Listen to the night

Forget everyday
This is what life should be

when we lay so close together
bodies touching
i don't know where my skin ends
and yours begins
and if I close my eyes
and clear my head
I can feel myself melt into you

i leave you with love
do not be afraid
it is not a binding love
but a love of what you gave to me

self esteem and confidence
believing that i am truly beautiful
physically/mentally (your words)

i will carry the fit of your body
and the music of the wind chimes
with me

another time, another place
here, now
where does the fantasy end and reality begin

let's not say those words "good-bye"
for there is no good in good-bye
let's just make love one more time
and believe it won't be the last.
leave me with a touch as i touch you back
smile that dirty chuckle
and let me think that i will make you laugh again.
and, if in time
we find that all we had was now,
may our memories serve us well
and make us smile again.

Another place (or here)
another time
Would I be yours
would you be mine

If we could meet in real time
on equal grounds together
Would it all seem as easy
as in island weather

Should we just take what we've been given
and slowly walk away
And hold the memories close at heart
and meet the brand new day

I must believe that we will know
what it is that we must do
And I will believe
that our hearts will see us thru

thanks for making me see that sometimes fairy tales do come true

I awoke early…as I would on the island
Even before I open my eyes
I know that something is missing…
the sound of the chimes

I come awake
and see a strange sky
this is gray sky…clouds…no sun

And silence…
no roosters crowing, no dogs barking
no ferry whistle
no chimes

And, I am alone
No touch to wake me
no one to roll into and become one…
I am home and I cry

I find my mind wandering to the what ifs of you and I
Are we both as cool as we appear
Or just afraid to say what's on our minds

What if instead of subtly inferring I love and want the island life
I'd said I want a real chance to get to know you
that I could help you run the business
work with you on fixing up the house

That I can be your partner, companion and lover
and that we can grow old together
and neither one of us would be alone again

Would that scare you
or would it release your thoughts and feelings
Are we both so careful to keep it light…
to keep it vacation time…island time

I wonder now that I am gone and I've had time to think
how you can limit yourself to only island women
(who have been passed around)
I wonder why you wouldn't look beyond a vacation fling
if you think there might be something there
Or are you happy just being cool and reserved
And taking your happiness wherever you may find it…
for the moment

it's been a long and lonely day
no touch to wake up to
saw no one today…
after spending a week with people every day
i feel very alone.

as the day wears on
i feel dead…
my thoughts slow down.

it's amazing to be with someone so much
and then to have nothing.
How can that be?
What are his thoughts?
What if they are the same as mine?

who is this man
with the smiling eyes
who makes me think
of a far off island
and renews my hope of love.

who listens when i speak
and already knows my body
like the back of his hand.

who is this man
with the delighted laugh
as he makes love to me
that I want to get to know.
who makes me think
I can still have my dream.

who's so easy to be with
and as comfortable as my favorite jeans.
with the island life I long for,
with the easy ways.
who will waft away
like the smoke from my ever present cigarette.

who is this man.
i must go slow
i must know what I want
before I can consider what he wants.

i know how to live life for the moment
i am grateful for any happiness i find
for all too often that is all i have

what i want is to go beyond the moment…
will that break the spell
and i'll be left with nothing

or, perhaps the time will come
when we each want more
and we will find that the moments can be strung together

and that happiness can be lasting

I am falling in love with a fantasy/dream
A quiet island life with a man
I don't even know
but think that I could live with

Help in his business
Rehab his place with him
Keep his house up
And he can keep me!

A simple life
Companionship/caring
mutual respect
and grow to love one another

Take a few years
to visit back and forth
and then be together
Want him to be dreaming this dream too.

Don't know if I should let my feelings go
Fall in love with you?
Live the dream?

Or settle for the status quo
My life is good
My future secure

But
if I walk away from this
it's never to return

And yet…as the years go on
I know that I want once more to love and be loved
and if that love is far away
and there is nothing to hold me here
why can I not go?
And love and dream?

Thoughts of you go thru my mind constantly
With a smile on my lips
you are my last thought at night
and when I awake the smile is still there
along with the thoughts of you

And then I think all day
The wonder of meeting you
The challenge it presents
My feelings…
do I let them soar
or keep them in check

Where can this lead
(anywhere we want)
Can I again change my life
(for it will be me that makes the changes)

Can I trust you with my love
with my life

Is this security I now own
worth keeping
Could I walk away
if you offer me love and my dream
I may wonder at all the questions
But I know the answer…
just ask me

Destiny?
is that who you are
have I met my soul mate?
Sometimes I feel it's true…
the way we are together

I've been here before
but somehow it was different
I don't feel the urgency
it's more a let's take our time and do it right
(THAT I've never done before)

I'm at peace with the thought of us
of the life I think we can share
The timing was right
And now it's time to take the time to make it right

Destiny!

I am so calm in this
You are so far away
with a life of your own
And yet I believe
we can grow into this.
We don't have to have it all NOW
There's no urgency
just a slow and easy let's get to know each other
Let's enjoy
let's be friends and lovers
Learn to trust one another
Learn to care
To be to each other what we have never been to another
To give unafraid
knowing we can lose nothing
Only gain each other

I've always imagined a house with no walls
I've dreamed of it and described it
Thought of building it

Little did I know it already existed
in a place I've dreamed of living
Simply waiting for me…
to come home

I want to write
My mind makes me dizzy
as the night closes in
the words come to me.

I want to live on that island
look out at the sea,
and as the night grows long
put down my words.

I don't want to lose them
I've so much to say.
Can I keep them together
til I find a way?

I sit here with my wine
wanting to call you
knowing it's too late

I sit here
missing you
only wanting you

I will sit here…alone
and be content
until I am with you again

Chapter 2

I return to the island and we ring in the New Year together...pure decadence.

Our days are slow and lazy...enjoying the pleasures of the island and each other. I find myself mesmerized and so in tune with the ocean. I feel it in my soul. I could walk the beach for hours alone with my thoughts and the beauty around me.

My thoughts of you are all over the board. I fantasize of a future not knowing what any of your thoughts are. You are not one to talk of your feelings, where I just babble on about everything (however, I am still careful in what I say). I am happy and willing to take some time with all of this.

In our time together we slowly learn the idiosyncrasies of each other. I find myself being the more forgiving and tolerant partner. We talk of compromise to make this work, but I wonder if you truly know the meaning of the word.

I wonder about all that I have worked for at home; the security I have made for myself. I know better than to give that up without a fair exchange. For now, I must move forward with my life, as hard as that may be.

a circle of thought
winds thru my mind
where are you
where am i in all of this
the circle continues and ravels
only to unwind
with words spoken by us
what do you want/what do i want
where do we go from here

The days pass too quickly.
How will I leave you when the time comes?
This is more than just "fun"
and I think we both know it.

Can we talk about it?
Can we speak about our feelings?
our hopes?
our fears?

I think we must.
For knowing whatever it is
is better than wondering.

Fantasy?
Reality?
can we put the fantasy to bed
and live with the reality
Please!

The sea is constant
wave upon wave hitting the beach
never ending
constantly changing
but always, always there

Can lovers be as the sea
as constant as the waves
staying in tune with the changes
never ending

I walk
and hear the heartbeat of the sea
A pulse that goes on endlessly
with each wave that meets the shore
The heartbeat of the earth

I walk
and its constant motion
puts me in tune with the earth
and my soul is now in rhythm with the sea

And so I walk
in tune with nature and myself

I feel your touch
And yet another day with you begins.
As I languish in your caress
I too reach for you,
For I have learned to give you the mornings.
In the wonderful haze of sleep,
Still not viewing the new day,
I bring you to your pleasure.
We lay satisfied in one another's arms…
And so the day begins.

it rains
a shower for the new day
to start the new year clean
to wash away the past

As the ferry pulls out
I look behind me and see the island
Then I turn
For I must look forward
Behind me are days of pleasure
Ahead is life
I must allow no room for sorrow
For there was no sadness in our days
I will come back to you
And we shall begin again

like a wave rolling in
the ocean brings me to you
and then takes me away again
as it rolls back out to sea

how many waves will bring us together
and then separate us

will our lives be as constant as the waves
bringing us back and forth?
or will we finally catch a wave
and roll with it?

His eyes are a beautiful blue
hair is salt and pepper (high blonde)
and so thick you can get lost in it.
His skin is soft and silky.
With love in my eyes I tell him he is gorgeous.
With a chuckle…in my head…
I think he is a walrus.

I fed him flan off my tongue on new year's eve
I took him in my mouth with champagne

I'm always topless at home…or naked
I love the look in his eyes when he looks at me

He has liberated me
He is my hedonism

He is my love slave
I am pure pleasure

We love to touch…always…anywhere
We talk constantly of sex

he tells me I'm beautiful
and I believe him

I make dinner naked
we eat naked
we clean up naked

he washes my hair
my body

he is overly polite
to me…to everybody
Is this how he keeps his distance?

And so now home
I'm sure I'll shed a tear
He'll act reserved on the phone
Life will go on
I'll adjust and be content
And look forward to February

Thank you my sweet

For the pure pleasure of being with you
for the mornings, afternoons and evenings
of giving ourselves to each other
and every moment in between

Away from you I will have my memories
I will close my eyes and feel your touch
and reach for you
and remember your eyes looking at me

And now I wonder…as you must too…
What next?
Where do you fit in my life?
And I in yours?

I'm falling in love with you
allowing myself to feel
you have given me hope
you don't say you care
but tell me in other ways

So, I dream
another visit
i will dazzle you
and hopefully we can talk
make plans for a future

do you know where you're going
how you feel
what you want

do you listen to your words
the hints they give me
the feelings they hint at

are you aware of your feelings
can you acknowledge them
and share them with me

i need more than a clue
i need something real
to hang on to

don't wait too long
to say the words
i need to hear

buried love will die
if smothered too long
never to reawaken

We have spent time in the sand
Long walks on the beach
in the early morning hours
A few hours on a lazy afternoon
sitting on the beach together
Comfortable in conversation or silence
just happy to be together
We have spent time together
loving, laughing, enjoying
the pure pleasure of being
And more time apart
yearning and waiting
to be together again
May the sands of time
bring us together
More often than not
til they separate us no more

Thinking of you
of me
of us
I vacillate on which path to take
Stay in my cold security
the comfort I have created for myself
my secure support of family and friends
a dream job with all the freedom I need
This life I have struggled to achieve
and have finally found peace in

Or to step off to the unknown of you
to open my heart and love
and venture out to a whole new world
Of you and me
sand and sun
and island life as only it can be

More and more I see my path
leading to the island and you
for I really believe that we
can have a full life together

I have a vision of us
as lovers and partners
knowing that we can laugh
and enjoy life together

(I do still wonder about the trying times…

could we work thru those too…
For life is not always sunny)

And for me…the island…
to constantly be in an atmosphere of nature
the sun, the sea, the breezes and rain
To marvel always at the beauty of it all
to not be shut away inside

My mind and heart are already there with you
I still struggle with the securities I feel I need
And yet with small encouragement from you
And a realistic discussion of the future

I would make a new path for myself…
to you
to us

will you join me in my dance of life
where we will find our own rhythm
and sing our own words
where we will each take time to lead
and learn new steps along the way
sometimes i will be the words
at others the melody
but always we will be in harmony
(and if at times we get off key
together we will find our way back to perfect pitch)
we will learn the beat of each other's heart
fall into a rhythm of love
waltz in sync thru our days
partners dancing to the tune of life

Let me in
I come to you
To learn the nuances of your life
And you only want to play
I understand this
But I need to see your life
The day to day humdrum of it
To see where I fit in
Then we can play
For the rest of our days

I see my days bringing
me ever closer to you
My life here slowly becomes
a means to get to you
Til the days here
are less than the time there
And then no more

Let's choose to grow old together
not because we need to...but want to
Let's throw away our doubts and fears
and give ourselves to this thing we've found
Let's look at the big picture
and fill it with just you and me
Let's promise ourselves to make it work
Doesn't that sound better
than going thru life alone
or with a string of short-term lovers?

i want to be in the same time zone as you for God's sake
where you don't start the day 2 hours before me
and end it in the same way

where we're talking about the same weather at least
and i can tell you about my day and you'll understand
where we have mutual friends and can be a couple

i want to hear your voice…not on the phone
see your smile and look into your eyes
kiss you and touch you…
begin and end my day with you

I'm realizing...
slowly
with sadness...
that this will never work...
at least not for me.

As much as I can see
a partnership and a good life...
a chance to live out some of my dreams...
i see no depth or substance.

I need more than chatter and casual sex.

once again i saw a chance for my dream
and i jumped in
but more cautiously
and as time goes on
i must slowly let go
for there is no depth to us
and i need more
the potential is there
for a good life
but there is no substance
to hold it together

My future lies in my hands
Not in dreams
that slowly fade away

oh to be young
and have my life in front of me
i would run to you in an instant
live out my dream
and know that when I woke up
the world would still be mine to conquer.

but
i am cautious now
for most of life is behind me
and security takes precedence over dreams
so I see no where for us to go
and slowly I let go of my dream

Chapter 3

I have become disillusioned…or more cautious…or afraid. I want so much for love to prevail but I am also afraid of my own feelings. And he is no help. He is so distant and does not know how to talk about feelings, wants and needs.

I listen to what he does say and try to make sense of it all. But I can only guess where he is really at. And so, my mind swims and my fears turn to anger and self preservation. And yet, I keep the dream alive.

I return again in March to celebrate our birthdays (as it turns out mine is never mentioned and his is a party). But, I only see what I want when I am there. I get caught up in him, the loving and the island. It is only when I return home that I can see the truth of it all.

But, I will not let go.

Once upon a time
When I could only find
My self esteem in the likes of you
When I had no self-respect or confidence
When my world revolved around a man
I would have run to you…
Given up my world
And all I had accomplished
To enter your world
And make it mine.

But now I know who I am
And rather than lose myself in you
You must commit to me
I will give
But you must give equally
No more the loss of self.

I am the exceptional woman
More than you have told me so
(and I know now without being told)

I have yet to meet the exceptional man
Oh, you are unique in some small way
But I will play on your mind forever

A bitter victory

i come to you with senses starved
and you feed me
the sight of you alone fills me
but there is so much more
your voice and laugh are like no other
you embrace me and my whole body responds
while my touching you only heightens the sensation
we are enveloped in the fragrance of our bodies
the taste of your kiss lingers
as I begin to hunger for you once more

I need

Love…to give and get…
companionship
a partner
humor
honesty
emotional support
understanding
concern
caring
compassion
trust
commitment
faithfulness

Will you hang in there
when the going gets rough

Can you share your life
can you let me in
can we truly be life partners

Can you accept my flaws
my imperfections
will you be there in the hard times

Can you truly make a commitment
not only to me...but to yourself
to see this thru forever
to not turn your back
when it's not all that you dreamed...
when reality sets in

Do you understand
that this is my life too
not just yours...
that we both have wants and needs

And that if we join together
it will not always be perfect
that sometimes we will fail...
but that we can recover

Do you know that love and commitment are work

a work of love…but work no less
that like a job…or anything else worth doing or having
it takes time and energy

That you are still an individual
but not alone
that in a relationship
your actions now affect us…not just you

That there will be hard times
when my wants and needs
will supersede yours…and the other way around

That the effort is worth it
for the greatest of these is love

Do you believe and want this enough
to make it work
to say I love you and want you
and back those words with actions
to make them have meaning
and to commit to the long haul
and make it work

Can I let my heart go
And release my feelings

How I want to say I love you
To believe and trust

Just thinking of the possibilities
Stirs my heart

I am ready to explode.

you see and want only the pure pleasure of life
and you see me as part of it
to fulfill your needs
and be the lady of your dreams

and I am pure pleasure
but you refuse to see
the other side of me
the bigger side of me
the pleasure comes with the whole package
something i'm sure you'll never accept

i sit quietly, lethargic to life…not moving
oh, my mind is active
thinking
i am so torn…
content in this life i have created
yet tempted by new possibilities
i feel in limbo…
do i choose my self-created security over love
is it fear of love and the unknown that makes me cautious
will i know which way to go
how do I make that life-changing decision
either way i'll never know the other side

miles of endless road before me
a winter sun following me
desolate fields roll by
and my thoughts are of you.

will my life's road end with you
the winter sun turn to caribbean sun
and the field harvest a life of love
and i will be with you?

we've yet to see where the journey ends
and if the sun will forever shine
we alone plant what the harvest will yield
alone or together

island castaway

living in the shadow of your frailties
not shunned by society
rather denying it
to live by your own rules
no questions asked…

you work and play
and go thru the motions
but when confronted with the uncomfortable
you shut down…

your island is your haven
nothing is expected
nothing is given
exiled by your shortcomings

island castaway

Tonite it ended for me
When we can't have a conversation
Because you can't deal with a topic
When you put up your defenses
And refuse to hear my concerns

I cannot deny my feelings
And you cannot face yours

i am heartbroken
yet unwilling to acknowledge it
another dream shattered by reality

how i wanted to love you…and i did
but your love only goes so far
and i am more

so, we are exiles
you on your island…i in my beliefs
together…alone

Dreams and thoughts of love die hard
Feelings cannot just be cast aside
It's all within reach yet cannot be

There's something missing
And that must be acknowledged
I cannot settle for only part of the dream

I want it all
Which is more than you can give
and now the dream will fade to a memory

you refuse to deal with unpleasantries…
my bad mood
forcing my fears and doubts
This is not your kind of conversation
Wanting only the free and easy
Ignoring the rest of it as if it doesn't exist
Only half of a relationship I say
And I want it all

love dies hard
and i was beginning to love you…
wanting to love you
that love would have brought me my dream…
or is it just a fantasy

i still believe there's something there
part of me wants to hang on
yet there is that doubt
that tells me it is not all there…
to cut my losses and move on

Dreams…attainable goals in another realm of life…extend yourself

Or

Fantasies…wishful thinking…unattainable flights of thought

I still want you
and what I saw we could have had
I am lured by the fun and easiness of you
and by the life I want for myself
But I cannot deny the whole of me
And you cannot accept me
so that leaves me torn
knowing I must be true to myself
I will sadly let you go

depression weighs me down
a thick blanket of depression
keeps me in bed
even tho saturday errands beckon me.
what has a hold of me
indecision about you?
lack of sex?
my approaching birthday?
my stagnant life?
i want to throw it off
and rise renewed
but that will not happen
til i work it out.

My body hungers to be touched
For a kiss…a caress
I need the nearness only sex can give
There is no one to love me
So I would settle for the physical act
(sad but true)
For a stranger's touch…a meaningless union
To feed me
Til I hunger again

I finally see you in the crowd
And I cannot get to you fast enough
Our lips meet and we wrap ourselves around each other
And the world stops.
This is all there is for the moment.
We are together again.

Who are you…
This man who knows so well how to satisfy me
Who I sleep so comfortably with
This man who I can spend a day working beside
To accomplish something together
This man that I am so comfortable with
Where being me is easy
This man who treats me fairly and with respect
This man who makes me feel beautiful
And tells me I am incredible
This man who shares his paradise with me
And makes me feel a part of it.

You are…
A decent human being
Honest in your dealings with others
And in your approach to your life
The man you are to me
Treating me with respect and caring
Accepting me for who and what I am
We have no "airs" about us
You are this man I love
For all that you give to me
For the person that you are
For all that we have shared

This love has no urgency
It asks nothing of you in return
This love does not consume

As others have
But rather makes my heart feel full
Accept this love graciously
And treat it kindly
This love is a gift
And you are free

Sun and sand and surf
And perfect timing
Brought us together

We have walked the beach hand in hand
Spent lazy afternoons soaking up the sun
Content with idle chatter or silence
Just happy to be together

Our times together can be measured
In loving, laughing and enjoying the pure pleasure of being
Time apart is counted
By waiting and yearning

May the sands of time
Forever flow
And continually
Bring us together

once again, sadly, i leave you
for i do not know how to stay
if i were younger…with all of life ahead of me
there would be no hesitation
if i were older…with all my mountains climbed
i would be there
how i would love to spend these years with you
but i am at the top of my game now
finally realizing what i have struggled my whole life for
how do i walk away when i am almost at the top
can we wait a few more years
and maintain a long distance relationship
or shall we be thankful for what we've had
and go our separate ways

it's all so anti-climatic
i knew i had to get home
and even wanted to
and now i don't want to be here

the flight was so long
i thought it would never end

i miss you
i just showered alone
i go to bed alone
who will touch me
hold me thru the night
awake with me in the morning?

felt i needed to be home
and i was ready to be back
to re-enter my world...
but now i am lost.

what's really important?
to live life alone?
to prove to myself i can do it?
no one cares but me.

Well, here I am
Back in my world
And you in yours.

What price freedom?

i climb into bed naked and alone
during the night i reach out
and find only a pillow for company
the windows are closed against the cold
the sounds are unfamiliar
i awake to a grey day
no sun in the sky
bare trees…the song of a lonely cardinal
i turn and find no caress to greet me
i am still alone

welcome home

Isn't love growing together
and caring to the point
that the tough stuff
isn't a hardship.
That you do
what needs to be done
'cause you wouldn't think twice
of doing otherwise.

My love…

i've been thru all the emotions
i've weighed heart and intellect
and i know that you are not enough.
your emotional distance…
the fish bowl of island life.
i have so much here…
all that you have rejected.
what you offer is not enough…
what we have together
will not see us thru.
a part of me will always love you…
but not enough.

Chapter 4

I have talked of buying a house in town and make the decision to move on with my life. You do not understand my need and desire for this move. Why I feel I must continue to move on. You do not understand that this is my life!

After the initial excitement of the move, I find no joy in my new home. It is much more demanding than condo living where everything is taken care of for you. I find myself resenting that we are miles apart, doing the same chores, when we could be together and cut our work in half.

You finally come to visit, a time together that is both wonderful and confusing.

I'm packed
All of my life in boxes
I survey it all in wonder
55 years old…everything I own in boxes.
If a stranger were to unpack it all
Would they discover the essence of me?

And so I move on
To another chapter of life
A house!
A new canvas
To express myself on.

May the journey never end.

i am finding this is not the life I want to be living
the house, the yard, the upkeep
i am finding no joy in it
perhaps it was something i had to have
to find out i didn't really want it…
be careful of what you wish for!

and you,
you are there, and i am here
sharing nothing but a few words a nite
feeling more and more that I am truly in love with you
and wanting what we can have together
not what i have apart from you

so i am finding no ambition, no desire
to fix and decorate and make my mark
on a place that is but a stopping point on my way to you
i think of your new place
and want to do it together with you
to make it ours
more and more i know that there is where i will find my joy

To myself…
I acknowledge my love for you.
The love came slowly…
acceptance slower.
But love can be denied only so long…
or it will die.
Now I work on accepting…
where that love will take me.

Each day I am acutely aware…
that in the near future
my world, as I know it will be gone.
My home, my job, my family and friends…
thousands of miles away.
While I…
am alone and adjusting to a new way of life…
new home, new job, new friends…
and you.

If it comes to be…
will you be patient with me as I adjust?
Can you show me love…
and support me emotionally…
til I find my way?

i sit in my world
and reflect on yours.
here I feel the same warmth of the sun
accompanied by lawn mowers, traffic and crows,
and remember waves rolling in, dogs barking and roosters.
here the earth is awakening with new grass, leaves and spring flowers.
will I miss the change of seasons and how they reflect on life?
my world is full and wonderful
yet missing something…
you.
we talk each night about our days,
we do the same chores miles apart.
couldn't we halve our work by being together?
can't our combined efforts bring us both prosperity?
how long will our fears of commitment and love keep us separated…
will our need for independence and fear of responsibility win out?
i think we both know where we're headed,
but we are not yet able to say the words.
are our separate lives really better than loving and sharing?
how much precious time will we let go by
separated because we fear love?

Think of it this way…
We're old enough to know what we want
and aren't going to take the time to play games.
Life's experience has been our teacher,
and tho we have baggage, it's not as heavy as it once was.
We've both taken time to live our lives freely…
no responsibility to another or commitment.
And now we are faced with love…
and the fear of it.
Will it be here for today, and then vanish?
Or do we fear our past mistakes and no longer trust our hearts?
Is our independence so important that we will forsake love?

We all have options…
And this is one of them.

We are at the crossroads of our relationship.
We both allude to our thoughts and feelings,
but never go into specifics.
Yet we both know it is time for discussion,
only for so long can we turn it over in our own minds.
No course can be set
Til we hear what the other's thoughts and feelings are.
Can we trust enough to speak our minds?
To share our feelings, our hopes, our dreams?
If there is to be a future, it starts now.

Are you the love of my life?
Perhaps it is so.
For I have found you at the time in my life
where I feel I have nothing more to prove.
I am no longer searching for me in someone else,
I am confident in who and what I am
and know that I can always make it on my own.

Ours is a life and love I want, not because I need it,
but rather choose to make my world bigger thru it…
by loving and receiving love.
Now I finally understand love,
and you are the love of my life!

Part of me says have this new life
who knows when love will find me again.
I'd like the semi-retired easy life
to work with you-write-time in the sun.

But what about island isolation,
My time with family and friends...
my time alone?
I want you but you cannot be everything.

I wonder if part of it for you is the anticipation of getting together.
Would you still think me incredible if I were there every day?
A relationship is like a job, it takes work to hold it together.
Or do you want just the easy parts of a relationship?

We could go on like this...but not forever.
Soon I will need to decide in which way to direct the focus of my life.
Whichever way that is
I know I will need to move forward.

As you so aptly put it last nite
we are on our way to our demise.
Another dream shattered.
I should have seen it,
and perhaps I did.
But once again, I dreamed too far.
It's not me who is letting go…
but you.
You who know how it should be
but can't make it happen.
You seem to focus on the negative of us
rather than to give the positive a chance.
You are so afraid of losing everything
when I want nothing but to love you.

When you rub your hand over hard, cold steel
remember the touch of my skin
as your hand glides over the curve of my hip.
Tell me that Washington
can look at you with love in his eyes
or spoon with you in bed at night.
The almighty dollar is your master,
that buys you fleeting moments of companionship
that you turn away from
when you may have to give of yourself.
In the end your success buys you nothing but solitude.

I sit here in my little patch of sun and wonder why…
why am I not there with you,
sharing a sun that always shines.
I try to focus on my life here and wonder why…
when in my mind and heart I am already there.

it is difficult to wait for someone else
to decide the course of my life.
for I am already gone from here.
my every action is focused on leaving…
yet I must wait for you.
so, at times I find myself angry,
feeling I am not in control of my own destiny,
living in a limbo of sorts,
with no direction.
as I wait for you…

I prepare for your arrival
by doing things I must…
dust, do the floors,
clean the bathroom,
laundry, shine the mirrors,
change the bed!
Shop… groceries, liquor, cigars,
Treats for you.
And all the while I am anticipating…
being in that clean bed with you!
Having a drink,
eating a salad out of the same bowl,
sleeping with you again.
And I can't help but wonder…
after all the talk this week,
will you make a decision,
will we shop for a ring?
Will we begin our walk on the same path?
The future!

when your world become so narrow
that it revolves around only you…
when you can see only one way to do things
and the only path to take is yours…
when you disregard another's view
before you even hear it thru…
when you've lost your desire to try something new
when your goals can only involve you…
when you've lost the ability to compromise
and see no need to share in life…
Love will be lost to you.

I hardly know me anymore.
When once everything had to be just so
I'm finding I no longer have time for perfection.
I look back on those years when I put myself and others thru hell
And wonder what it was all about.
Proving to myself that I truly was a super woman?
Now I find myself wanting more time for me…
To read, to write, to travel, to visit with friends.
I cannot live in chaos
But time is too short to honor perfection.

My hopes, my dreams, my plans, my love…
I put in your hands to become ours,
and you gave them back to me.
I had too much to give
And you did not know how to accept it.
What you had to give
you chose to keep to yourself.
Now I leave you empty-handed.

who will i be in a year
or two or ten?
for that matter
who will you be?
what will life bring us in those years?

for we will change
as will life,
nothing stays the same…
and that is as it should be.
we cannot foresee the future
i know I love you now
i want to love you then.

I can make it thru my days
without thoughts of you driving me nuts…
the work day more than keeps my mind occupied.
It is in the evening when thoughts of you take over.
Now that we have put ourselves into this limbo
all I do is question why.
Why do we feel it easier
to walk away from something we may never find again
Than to find a way to keep it going and make it work?
Isn't it sad that fear is the motivation
and cannot be overcome?

What will life be like
When your voice is no longer a part of my day?
When there will be no more walks on the beach
Or dinner and drinks shared together?

What will life be like
When I know your touch will not be there?
When we will never share a bed together
Or wake up to a long, sensual shower?

What will life be like
When you are only a memory?

love is never mentioned
but we speak of our demise.
for it is easier to walk away from all that is good
than to face our demons.
we are willing to work at success measured in monetary gain
but will put no effort into a meaningful relationship
that would make the circle of life complete.

time has passed so fast since we met
will it be so when we are no longer together?
with nothing to look forward to
will the days and weeks drag on?
who will we share our news of the day with?
will the nights seem longer?
Perhaps…til another takes my place and the memories slowly fade.

My mind reels with thoughts of you…of us.
With the beginning of the end
we are choosing to walk away
from something that has been good from the start…
and has only gotten better.
May we never ask – what if

a chance meeting...a drink.
sunset on the deck...dinner
waking to you the next morning.
and it just kept going...getting better.

there was never an awkward moment,
no time for self-consciousness...
from sleeping together comfortably
to morning showers,
coffee and juice,
breakfast on the veranda,
work time, beach time, our time...
all happened naturally.

phone calls, plans to get together,
sharing our lives from a distance,
feelings we only hinted at,
fears to overcome...
but always moving forward.

how does something so natural and easy...
end so suddenly?

I leave you now.
My heart hurts.
I have no words now.
Time will sort this out.
Words will come.
I will write.
And I will heal my heart.

Your leaving takes my breath away.
With you goes my joy
the smile on my face
the light in my eyes,
both gone.
My arms are empty
my lips long for a kiss
as my body yearns for your touch.
You take my heart and love with you
handle gently
til we meet again.

Obviously,
Love is not enough.
We chose to walk away from it
in the name of security and independence.
Yet,
we will continue to search
for exactly what we have found.

Chapter 5

Each time I return to the island, my heart is full of hope and my head is knowing better.

Our times together, as always, are filled only with us…for time together is so short. We do finally speak of love and my hope is renewed. When again apart, our conversations bring reality back…my frustrations rise. Yet when I return to you on the island it all melts away. I am on a roller coaster of emotions.

once again i am on my way to you
my mind reels with thoughts of you
what will i actually tell you about how i feel
how will you react
where will it leave my thoughts and feelings

right now i feel i need to say i can't do this anymore
that if you can't commit
i need to move on with my life
that you pull my heart strings back and forth
and my emotions don't know where to land

and yet, as i get nearer to you
my heart sings

i have no answers
only thoughts and questions
i feel that I'm on a roller coaster
and i want off

We come together
and the music starts
Our bodies are the instruments
finely tuned to each other

The words come slowly
a kiss, a caress
Unspoken poetry
our eyes meet, a smile

As we join together
the silent composition is complete

Now that we have spoken of love
my heart is free to feel.
No more denying emotions
that are meant to be felt.

I can go now
knowing that there will be more.
And believing that in time
our love will conquer all.

Think of me…of us
and all that we can have.
I promise you, if given the chance
it will only get better.

we sit silently
and watch the sunset
each with our own private thoughts
i rest my head on your leg
you play with my hair
and i want to hold the moment forever

the sun falls behind a cloud
hidden as our thoughts are
it will show itself again
will we?

you are my love
i look at you
in wonder and awe
that a chance meeting
could come to this

will you be my love?
let me live my dreams with you
and i will make yours come true

once again we part
we sit silently
where do your thoughts take you
then an all encompassing hug
that speaks all we do not say
i watch you walk away
and i wonder why it must be this way

What is it like after I leave?
As you take out the garbage
and throw away traces of me
You put two cereal bowls away…
which one was mine?
The wine glasses on the shelf…
will they be used again before I return?
Does the shower seem bigger…
and empty?
Close your eyes and let the water be me…
caressing you.
Will you crawl into bed on our sheets…
smelling the essence of me…
reaching out and coming up empty handed?
Is this how the void begins?

i feel this is our turning point
that now time apart will be more intense
that time together will not be enough
that given time
it will take us
on the course we have already set

a writer without a pen
is like the sky without a star
an ocean with no tide
a rainbow with no color

with no pen
the words cannot appear
locked in the mind
with no release

Think about it long and hard
and I will too.
No more anticipation
or sending me home…
the void will be permanently filled.
I will be your constant companion.
You will wake to me
spend your days with me
and then your nights.
We will work together
play together, love together.
Work things thru
and grow old together.
Think about it long and hard
and I will too.

Eventually we will have to believe.
You ask for extended time together.
I say it will prove nothing.
But…
If that is what you feel you need
I will find a way to give it to you.
In the end what will be needed
Is a leap of faith.

Listen. Don't make a sound.
Just stand silently as one.
With arms around each other
we melt into one.

Listen. Hear without a word.
We speak to the essence of one another.
With arms around each other
our souls meet.

Listen. Closely.
For our hearts are speaking,
telling us of love.

i contemplate my life
and where i am going
knowing that i am in suspension
til you decide my fate

my frustration reaches a crescendo.
i must find a way to contain it.
i am not one to dally in life's nuances,
but rather to forge ahead.
you, on the other hand, are stuck.
and your ways flame my frustration.
in younger, reckless days
i'd be impetuous,
but now I sit,
contain myself,
and wait.

If giving up the game
still means something to you,
then you are not ready to be with me.

If the thought of conquest
and the excitement of the first encounter
is still something that you crave,
then you are not ready to be with me.

If it's important, as you grow older,
to be the roving bachelor,
then you are not ready to be with me.

You'd think the game would grow old,
the conquests become less frequent,
as an old man you may be lonely.

You see, I will not play the game.
Our first encounter is over.
And if it's important to forever be the Casanova,
then you are not ready to be with me!

Will you miss looking around the corner
for what comes next?
On an island there is always
the next lonely tourist
looking for that easy week long affair.

If you settle for me now
will you always wonder what you missed?
Can you grow old with me
and be content?
Can real love make you happy,
or must you have the constant pursuit and conquest?

My children…
Do not think I am abandoning you,
or make me feel guilty.
You will always be my first loves,
and always I will be there for you.
Perhaps not as much physically
but always there.

Try to be happy for me
in that I have found my love
and can live my dream.
That I will have the opportunity
to work and write
and live life leisurely.

Respect this man who loves me,
who respects my love for you,
and encourages me in my pursuits.
Tho he takes me away
I am always with you,
Loving you as only I can.

come…

let's go to bed
and make sweet love

as we undress
we reveal the pleasures to be had

lay down beside me
our bodies touching head to toe

hold me close
til there is no more knowing that we are two

there are no words needed
for our eyes and lips and hands are speaking now

as we discover each other anew
with a sigh and a smile

we are one

On the beach
I sunbathe
Laying there
Soaking up the sun
Hearing the waves crash to shore
Oblivious to the rest of the world

As I open my eyes
I see the sky…
Or is it?
For the wispy clouds
Look like the breakers on the ocean
As the world is turned upside down

You are my love,
eight months and running,
I want it to never end.

Tell me what you need,
and be sure
I will give it to you.

Believe that it can only get better,
and it will.
Be my love, forever.

i sit on your patio at night
alone and naked
and the breeze becomes my lover.
as it blows thru my hair
i lift my face to catch it's gentle caress.
as it touches my eyes
and kisses my lips
it slowly glides
over my breasts
as gentle as a lover's hand.
it travels down my stomach
imitating loves little kisses
until it reaches my most private place
and gently laps at me.
a sensuous lover
that never intrudes.

Sound asleep
I am awakened by your touch.
I respond
as my body thrills to your love.
And so the day begins.

Island days
where you wake up to a clear day
the dogs barking, roosters crowing
the sun shining and the vastness of the ocean greets you

Days and nights fighting off mosquitos
where sweat pours down your face while working
where the rains appear from no where
and just as suddenly are gone

Where life is slow
time is my own
and the days blend together

i want you to say yes
and still you hesitate.
i know the reasons why
and even appreciate them…
this is both of our lives we are talking about.

yet, i want to get on with it,
to start the journey
that will end with our being together
and then begin our journey.

Once more I leave you,
this time not knowing
when we will be together again.

Think hard my love,
for the parting does not get easier.
The days apart are wasted time,
and even yes means 6 more long months apart.

I may be gone
but my heart remains with you.
I will be whole again
when next I am with you.

i leave you now
but the bigger part of me stays here
my love for you lingers
as does the yearning for the sea and sky
what a life we can have
do not deny me
you are my dream
my love

sometimes i'm not sure about you
where you're at or what you're thinking
about all of this.
and then i get scared
and unsure of myself and you
i worry that i cling too much
and bug you with my silly innuendoes
when really i don't worry
i believe that you will come thru
and if not I will survive

The marrying kind?
That seems to be our downfall.
You'd have me now
except i will not come
until you are the marrying kind.

You respect my demands,
yet those same demands
may end it all.
It's not a question of love.
But, are you the marrying kind?

How many times
must you see me go
before you ask me to stay?

Does not the joy
go out of life
the moment that we part?

Have we not
had the signs
that this is meant to be?

What more
is there to life
except for you and me?

Don't defy the gods,
For they have sent
A message from the sea:

A perfect heart
a lover finds
washed upon the shore.
The Gods are speaking
it's a sign
we'll be together ever more.

An unusual find,
It must be a sign
That in years to come
You will be mine.

In the course of thinking this thing thru
remember there is the distinct chance
we will never find this again.
In your mind, go over past relationships
and figure out why they have failed…
Who were you then…what were you looking for?
And then see who you are today,
where you're at and where you are going.
Is a life alone your goal?

i am learning patience
how much time in a day
do i spend waiting for you

to take a shower
to eat
or to leave to go somewhere

i do not let it bother me
i've slowed my pace
knowing that when i am finally here
i too will have my thing to do

You know
You're never going to find
anything like this again.
We sing the song
and dance the dance.
And the melody continues
as we learn new steps…
From recognizing each other's moods
to knowing which buttons to push.
To sexual pleasures yet unexplored.
Neither of us has ever had this before…
it's not likely to be found again.
Think about it.

today i have an uneasy feeling...
don't know where it's coming from
but i feel things have changed.
i don't know what that change is
but i know i have to talk with you about it
i need to know from what it stems.

I Love You

just words
until you give them life

I love you.
From sunrise to sunset to sunrise again.
I love you.
Thru good days and bad days and back to good again.
I love you.
No matter where I'm at or where you are
I just love you.

Are things changing?
Is my gut telling me something
my heart does not want to know?

I detect subtle differences,
that you are not fully there.
that perhaps you are thinking differently.

But I don't know where it's coming from,
Or how it started.
Please return to me.

listen as you walk along the beach
and you will hear the earth breathe
as the sea takes a breath
it slowly exhales as the wave rolls to shore
and the foam lets out a sigh
as another breath is taken.

And so we part
with hugs and kisses
with words of love.

Make this all go away.

Chapter 6

And so it goes. Each visit buoys me up while time apart is filled with my doubts. Still I yearn for my dream to come true.

Is it that I believe in this love so much or that I want the dream? I cannot distingush between what my heart feels and wants and what is in my head.

Where do the feelings come from?
All of a sudden I feel that I am losing.
Why?
I tell myself it is just me…
but I know it's not.
My gut feelings are trying to tell me something.
I asked if all was well as we walked the beach.
You assured me it was
and I relaxed.
But,
It's back again…
That fear in the pit of my stomach.
Nothing I can put a finger on…
just something as a woman I feel.
I feel decisions have been made
that have not been told to me
because you know it is not what I want to hear.
How can I bring it up again?
You just won't tolerate it.
And now that I think about it
maybe the difference is me.
I'm more ready to leave…
I want the process to begin.
I'm tired of waiting..
Is this the reason for my feeling this way?
Knowing that I will just have to wait it out.

What is this feeling that I can't shake?
This subtle difference in things that I detect?
The feeling that you are slipping away from me
making me realize how much I love you.

Does woman's intuition kick in
when our heart rules?

You know…
I would give up my whole life for you.
But there is going to come a point
when I say no more.
I've done all that I'm going to do
and you must decide what you want
and I will live with it.

You say that we are both survivors,
and that's true.
But I'm beyond that point in my life
where I just want to survive.
I know what I want.
Tell me where you're at
and I will go from there.

When are we going to stop living like this!
i go to a family picnic…
you go to a wedding…
And then we share our lives over the phone!

Don't you want to experience things together?
To go places as a couple?
To truly share life together?
To make memories together?

I'm so tired of this…
in a relationship lived thousands of miles apart,
living for the next conjugal visit!
I want more!

Can we please just get past
living separate lives
in different parts of the world?

How long are we going to go on
sharing our lives over the phone
rather than sharing experiences together?

This has to be some sort of limbo for you
as much as it is for me…
I want to live my life to the fullest!

I know that you are struggling
to make some sense of all of this…
but don't we need to move forward?

There is no one thing that will define the path…
there is no foreseeing the future…
there is only believing in ourselves, one another…
our love

You know our faithfulness to each other
and our level of trust in one another
says a lot about our commitment to each other.

A long distance relationship is not an easy thing
and yet there has never been a question of commitment
i have truly never worried about what you are doing
i couldn't handle that
and you need not worry about me

Think about it…
what it says about each of us individually
what it says about us together in a relationship
what it says of our feelings for each other

Love is a strange and mysterious thing
You never know when it will tap you on the heart
Or where it will lead you when it does.

When we think we have our lives all figured out
It makes us think again
And realize just how much fuller life can be.

Love is not always easy
It requires scope and vision…
Of places not yet visited.

But love is rewarding
To give and receive, to share one's life
It's a whole new world when lived together.

i would say i love you
more than life itself…
almost

i will leave my children (and grandchildren) behind,
(which will change that relationship),
not to mention my job, friends, family and lifestyle,
but what we have together is so special
i don't think i've ever had this before…
or will find it again

we have an ease about us…
from sex, to showers, to meals
just day to day is easy
and has been from the start

so my love for you is great…
i tease…but i'm glad we've taken our time…
and i believe our love will win out

I love you
in so may ways
for so many reasons.
That we make love
at the end of the bed
playing
laughing afterwards.
Holding hands
never sitting across the table from one another.
Phone calls
getting to know each other.
Getting naked in the kitchen
the car, going up the stairs.
Picnics
the beach
you under a tree
me walking the beach.
Your pleasure in watching me
play in the waves.
How you worry about me
that you are more cautious than I.
You make me feel loved and cared for
and beautiful.
Our little routines
are you ready yet.
The things that you have taught me
to love again
patience.

he looks at me naked
and makes me believe that i am beautiful

I'm here again
where I belong
Traveled all day
just to get here
The closer I got
the more I wanted you
Seeing you standing there
waiting for me
That first embrace
made everything worth it

We talked at dinner.
The look in your eyes.
The smile on your face.
No words…

i'm 55 years young
lying on a bed in the caribbean
watching a 60-year-old man
hang wind chimes
in a one room kitchenette
he's going to live in
while he rebuilds his home
and i am happy
i wish i could stay here with him
for the rest of my life

almost "home"
can't believe that once again
we are apart

Sometimes you scare me
and I wonder what you're saying
"between the lines"
I wish you could just talk about your feelings
and your thought process in all of this
But I know that isn't you
So I wait you out
knowing better than to push
But aching inside
with the uncertainty you leave me feeling

Again we have not touched for a month.

Greet me at the airport
Kiss me
Hold me
And take me home.

Get me naked and caress me
With your eyes
Your hands
Your lips.

Lay with me
And let me feel your body next to mine
Let's explore each other
As if it were the first time.

Let's awaken every desire
Then join together
And consummate our love.

It has been said:
"into each life some rain must fall"
There are reasons for the rain,
without rain we could not see the beauty of a rainbow
or truly appreciate a sunny day.
Which is saying life is two-sided
the negative accentuates the positive.
How would we know a good day
if there was never a bad day.
Ill health reminds us to take care of ourselves
sorrow and loss remind us of our mortality
and to live life to the fullest.
Highs are the best…but without a low
we wouldn't know a high when it came along.
Like true love…
perhaps to recognize it
we first have to fail at love…
live an empty life…
to appreciate the gift we have been given.

Tread softly
the heart is fragile
Love is strong
but can only bend so far
Learn to give
that which you want to be given
Give love life
By giving your life to love

You know…

i've gotten to the point
where all i want is an answer
and i really don't care what it is

i've learned to play your game
i know what buttons to push
and which to stay away from
i wish i could say that you know the same about me

i don't mind giving
but i need something back
i "treat you good" just doesn't cut it
not for the long term anyway

you need to learn to give back
that which you expect to receive

I guess I need to acknowledge
that perhaps I'm having doubts.
I believe that you love me
but are you so needy
that you can't see that I have needs too?
I have no problem loving you
caring about you
pampering you.
But if I am not nourished by you
I will be drained.
There will be nothing left for me to give.
I want us so badly.
But not at the expense of me.

just give a little
pamper me a pinch
listen to what i say
share what you do
i ask so little
and you'll receive so much

You get so defensive,
there's no need for that.
I'm not attacking you!
I'm only trying to explain my feelings.
Listen to what I say
and you'll learn so much.
It can all be so easy
if you accept what we have.
You are not losing anything
but gaining everything!

I'm sure you love me
and want a life together.
I know you've weighed
all the pros and cons
and that they lean
to the pro side.
So it seems to me
your fear holds you back
and your procrastinating ways.
Which for your information
can only take precedence for so long.
We really are old enough
to know what we want.
If you choose to be stuck
in your idealism
i will have no choice but to live by my reality
and move forward with my life.

in the autumn of my life
i watch another summer waning
gone the long sultry days
that warm my soul
and make me feel alive
even now there are days
that hint of what is to come
falling leaves
then cold and snow
darkness that comes
before the day has ended
already i begin to yearn for spring…
as i enter the autumn of my life.

Chapter 7

As I reflect on my life I know that my youth is over and that I now have less time to accomplish my goals than all of the years I have already lived. With the events of 9-11 life becomes more precious and time too short.

As 9-11 unfolded it touched my life in ways yet unknown. You were there and I was here and there was no way to get together. This played havoc on our relationship. I selfishly wanted and needed to be with you while I felt guilty. Others were suffering…and I was in love.

And while you procrastinated in your island paradise my doubts and fears grew as your selfishness became more apparent.

We hurry thru our lives…
There's not enough minutes in an hour
hours in a day
weeks in a month
or months in a year
We try to cram so much into the time we are given
That we hardly notice what we've done or what we have.

It's true that youth is wasted on the young.
For while we have all those years of freedom
We do not yet have the experience to enjoy them;
By the time we do realize what youth holds
We are no longer young.

Now we are looking at our children
And wishing they could stay young forever;
Alas, their fate is as ours.
Our children grow and mature
And we find ourselves in our twilight years
Realizing in our rush thru life
We've never taken the time to live a dream…
To love completely…
Or to be the person we set out to be
So long ago
When there was still time.

A day of terror
That puts fear into our country
As America shuts down.
No airplanes flying
Stock market closed
As well as businesses, schools, shopping centers.
An eerie quiet settles over us.
We sit glued to the television
Unable to comprehend
That this can happen on our soil.
In days to come
We will learn the full magnitude
Of lives lost
And changed.
And where we go from here.
We now know the fear
Of being attacked
Of being vulnerable.
God help us all.

first i tried to contact my children…
to talk with them and know they are okay.
then i found you
knowing that you would not know
that we had been attacked.
shaking with fear
i tell you the events of the morning.
you are outraged…as we all are.
i think we both realize
our need to be together
and that it has been made clear
that life is too short.

Today in the wake of fear
I realize my mortality in another way
Not in health issues or old age
But attack and war
A fear that I have never known before
A fear worse than health and old age
And I realize that my plans and goals
Can be taken away by others
More than ever
I believe now we must live our lives
To make our love a realization
Do not put off what is available today
For it can all be gone tomorrow

our skies are quiet…
no plane has flown for 36 hours
an unknown stillness fills the land
a vital part of our lives is missing
beautiful days with blue skies
yet no jet clouds to be seen
no air traffic noise to complain about
(will we appreciate it later)
no flights to watch go over and dream of far away places
also the fear of being grounded…
when can i plan to leave again
our country at a standstill
our lives changed
we must never forget the silence
or allow to be silenced again

In these frightening times
Is it wrong to wonder when I will see you again
It feels selfish
In the wake of all who are suffering
To want to know when we can again be together
In some ways this has brought home to us
The need to be together
How much better we would both feel
If we were not now thousands of miles apart

What if…we never see each other again.

I see the pictures
Hear the pain
Feel the fear
Try to understand
What has happened
To this country
Our freedom
My life
What next…
Does life return to normal?

I sit in front of the TV
I could sit there forever
See what I've seen before
Heard it all
Yet I cannot tear myself away
I don't think it's all set in yet
At least not for me
I watch and listen
As my chest swells and tightens
What will we call normal after this?

the weather's changing…
cool mornings, cooler evenings
with warm days in between
a hint of fall in the air
daylight is shorter
windows close
jackets come out
leaves change color
and fall to the ground
blankets are needed
as summer departs
and fall sets in…
my mood darkens

Selfishly I hurt for myself
and am angry that my own little world has been affected
Angry that strangers…in a moment of violence…can touch my life
On a larger scale
I hurt for all who are suffering…
who have lost loved ones
And I fear for our country…and the world
I pray that those who plan evil will pause…
and think beyond their personal hate
For by striking America they doom their own world…
and all of the world

This isn't fun anymore
I should be in love and happy…
looking forward to the future
Instead, as I play your game
and wait for your decision
I find myself becoming negative about the whole thing
I have no clue as to where your head is at…
you give me no reassurance
yet you expect it
We are not kids
we've both been around the block a few times
By now we should know what we want out of life
I want to feel like I'm in love…
giddy and excited
I'm ready to start planning our life together…
I can't live in limbo much longer

for wanting only the highs in life
you are awfully pessimistic...
rarely seeing the good in a situation

you find your humor funny
but have difficulty in understanding mine...
when was the last time you laughed til your sides hurt

if life is to be lived only on the high side
where is the laughter...
the silliness...the sense of adventure

you are a procrastinator by nature
which hinders your moving forward in life...
is there nothing you wish to accomplish

you create your own stress
with the lifestyle you have chosen

oh you of fragile spirit
who thinks himself so strong

can i forever bolster your ego
and keep things right between us

how long can i deny myself
to live in the sun
within the shadow of your needs

do not quell my spirit
for you are killing a part of me you love

and when you have contained me
you will no longer love me

you drive me away
with your narrowness
why do i seek you
when another makes me laugh
and takes life easily

your island is your refuge
but you cannot hide from yourself
i ask for things you have buried
and now fear to look at

you will not find another me
take stock of yourself
and decide to hide if you must
knowing this will not come again

whether you know it or not
whether you ever acknowledge it…
i am the love of your life
i have brought more to your life
than any other woman has ever given you
it is your choice to accept me or not
if your fears are stronger than your love for me
you will go your singular way…
and remain there
in days and years to come
I will haunt you…
No one will compare
And you will search for what we had
For all the days of your life

Does another dream come to an end?
Will the pain be intolerable?
What is next in life?

How can a man be so pigheaded?
Putting words in my mouth
Only hearing what he wants to hear
Again not listening as I try to explain
Refusing to hear what I say…
And let it go

I'm sure you feel your manhood was assaulted…
Which it wasn't

Your insecurities are immense
Your ego even more so

Is this all a warning sign?

i am stronger than you
and will survive the storm of our love
i will persevere
while you wallow
and betray yourself
with truths known only to you
tho i will regret our demise
i will not allow your spirit to haunt me

there will be another love and i will survive!

turmoil at work
keeps us apart
do you really understand
or is your disappointment
based only on your needs

island life
has made you forget
what real responsibility is
and i'm not sure
if you understand true friendship

others have come before you
before us
i think you find
this hard to deal with
are you always first

and my life…right now
must be my central focus
where does that leave us
where are you
what are you thinking

Chapter 8

My mind and heart are at war. Because of world events we have not seen each other for an extended period of time, and it is taking its toll on us. I plan another trip, and it too, is cancelled, this time because of happenings at work. Being who he is he is not able to understand my life here. He cannot be supportive of what is going on in my life. His needs are not being met; he does not know how to discuss it and will not listen to what I have to say.

As things deteriorate I still cannot let go of love. I have hit a brick wall and have no where now to go and yet I continue…wanting my dream til the bitter end.

we fought last night
and i haven't heard from you today

a friend came over
and we took up
where we left off a year ago
we talked...and laughed
and it all felt good

i talked with a girlfriend
about a vacation in november
i'm scheduling things
to get my life in shape

it's the first day
of the rest of my life
and i feel good!

you have tumbled me
as the sea does glass
alone now…
having loved and lost…
i take on a new form
and go forward

I'll miss the island
(maybe more than you)
the beaches
to sit and feel the sun rejuvenate me
the timeless lap of the waves…
never ceasing
the walks alone…
to ponder life

my dreams of life with you
took me away from here
but now that dream is shattered
and i feel i can focus again
it is time to re-group
and to make goals
to be happy with what i have
and who i am

I knew this was coming
even before you did.
I knew it wasn't going to work.
But I kept hoping you'd come around.

We could compromise
but you won't.
And I can't live my life by your rules.

I tried so hard
to make us okay.
But I couldn't do it by myself.

i sit at night and think about you
knowing it's over
knowing it's for the best

but i still wonder
what we could have done differently
do you

to have had so much
and to now have nothing

the feelings don't go away easily
they will linger for a long while
and a piece of my heart will be yours forever

is this how it ends
with a phone conversation on a Monday night?
never to speak again?
no face to face closure?

we didn't even realize the last time we made love
was to be the last!

i have so much i want to say to you
yet know that it would be useless…
you wouldn't hear what i was saying
or understand

did we both want this so badly
that we fooled ourselves for all of this time?

it's time to re-group
and start living my life again
i need to look at where i am at
and figure out where i want to be
i'm starting a whole new journey again…
let's go

keep the house?
if yes – refinance?
and…
fix the yard?
cut down the tree?
door handles to put on
faucets to replace
put in a dishwasher?
then new countertops?
buy rugs
paint cabinets
decorate

You know…
I'd be sitting here alone anyway
so nothing has really changed…
Except I don't hear your voice anymore
Your touch is gone forever
and your kiss will soon become a memory
How long will it be
before I can no longer remember the look in your eyes…
or your smile?

I can still feel your caress
and know what it is like to be with you
All is gone
except the hole in my heart

another dream is shattered
another love is lost

perhaps it is time to dream a dream
i alone can make come true…

and then find love

How I will miss the island!

I was comfortable there.
So in tune with the rhythm.

To sit and watch the sea and write.
To wake to the island noises.

Oh, the beaches…
to walk endlessly and feel free
to lay and feed on the sun
the endless waves calming me.

The full moon on the water
countless stars in the sky
night breezes caressing me.

Even the sudden rain
to fall upon my face.

Where will I find this again?

your motto
no live plants
no children
no pets
just close the door and leave.

add to that
no self-realization
selfishness and a big ego
an inability to nurture
and the door closes behind you.

are you alone?
drinking at home?
or out drowning your sorrows?
are you angry?
or hurt?
or just feeling your freedom returned?
have you found another…
to lose yourself in for the moment?
(and did you think of me?)
are you questioning?
thinking?
i never did know where you were at.
do you?
does it matter?

so this is how it ends.
i won't call
and you probably won't either.

as quickly as we came together…

we part.

Sometimes you just pop into my mind
and I think about how much I love you
My chest just fills up
I wanted what we had together so much
I can't believe it's over
Just the wrong phone conversation
and you're gone
how can that be

Am I haunting you too?

finally called you tonight
and i feel good about it
didn't like the way things were happening with us
that's not the way i do things

we spoke hesitantly-quietly
not much reason to discuss what got us here…
just where to go now

neither of us knows
where our relationship is right now
but we do agree we're not ready for it to be over

back to square one

Love does not go easily.
Tho the heart hurts
it will not give in.
So we will try again…
still in love…
always cautious

Now I reprioritize
Tho still in love and wanting you
My first commitment must be to me
My life here will now take precedence
as it should
My goals will center on what I know I have
getting ahead in my job
making my house my home
providing for my future
Being content with the life I make for myself
Rather than dreaming of a life with you
that may never be

and what of the man who makes me smile?
who with the sound of his voice
on my worst day,
can make me laugh?
who understands my wit
who's still a bit afraid
but interested enough to come back after a year
knowing that we both care
and that he's taking a chance
at what he was afraid of before
it's certainly worth
taking a second look

i'm learning to appreciate my life here again
i've been so negative…thinking that i'd soon be living on the island
but, as that is not to be,
it's time to start seeing the beauty of my life here
the crisp fall air with bright/clear sunshine
(the sunsets more striking than any i've seen on the island lately)
the trees dressed in their fall colors
the woodpecker at my kitchen window
there are joys and beauty that surround me
if i only take the time to see and appreciate

your whole premise is
you live on a caribbean island and life is beautiful
when in fact
you live on a caribbean island
and your life is just like mine
you may deal with life's trials and tribulations
where the sun is constantly shining
and you look out at the sea
but the climate does not dictate life's flow
the joys in life are not brought on by the sun and sea
but by who we are and how we deal with life
you are just as alone there as i am here
struggling to make meaning out of life

my house takes on new meaning now
as i walk thru its rooms
it begins to feel like home

and what of this old love
who, with the sound of his voice
can make me laugh even on my worst day
he's sniffing around again
and I'm sniffing back…
laughter is the best medicine

Do you ever wonder why?
I hate to say what if.
Time will tell gets old.
So does que sera sera

Maybe why is supposed to mean something.
And what if we make time tell?
And aren't we responsible for what will be?

And what about fate…
don't we have a hand in that too?

We're speaking again…not every day
but occasional unplanned calls…
taking tentative steps at starting over.

And I find myself redefining…
This has been good for me…this stepping back…
I have reclaimed my life here
and am searching for what I want from you.

I will ask you to listen (to hear) what I have to say…
to curb your anger at what you hear…
to not become defensive.

And, while listening, to concentrate on what I say…
not on formulating your response.
I will not ask you to agree with my thoughts and feelings…
but to accept them as part of me
and to thoughtfully consider if they will fit into your life.

the sea glass necklace i wear around my neck
is a symbol of our love
it also speaks of broken things
made into something new
once whole
then smashed against the shore
sharp edges to be tumbled away by time
to be recreated and given new meaning.

you need to know i will wait for you…
but not indefinitely
i love you…
but i want love and companionship more than one weekend a month
if i were looking for just a lover
i could surely find one closer to home!
i want to share my life with someone…
be together every day thru life's ups and downs
someone there to share my joys and tears
i don't want to sleep alone every night…
eat meals alone…
celebrate holidays alone
i don't want to work on my separate goals…
alone
while you work on yours

it is sad but true
as the saying goes
that your saying no
(one little word)
set me free to live my life again.

i am now bonding to my new home
feeling it is my palette to express myself.
my writing is coming together
i find i can write whether looking over the caribbean or not
i'm finding a new joy in all that is familiar…
that i had turned my back on since you.

What I am realizing is…
It is not where you are at
But where you are within…
that matters.

perhaps when you see me again
you will wish you would have reconsidered
or then again
i may re-enforce your decision.
either way I've changed.
my dreams must once again revolve around me
and perhaps rightfully so.
put in your hands they lost their high…
in mine they shall soar!

The skies are alive again
but the sounds are different.
No more just commercial airliners
bussing business men and pleasure seekers.
Now you hear the distant sounds of fighter jets,
and military helicopters,
protecting both those in the air and on the ground.
Troubling sounds,
that produce a fear
and make you aware
that life has forever changed.

it has occurred to me
that you are so consumed with the fear
of yes being a mistake
that you have never considered
that the opposite may be true

He doesn't call.
Rather than deal with any kind of confrontation
he will remain silent.
And, in his mind, he will make it right.
I don't understand the demons that control him.
If this is love to him
how can he just let it fall apart?

i wonder sometimes
if it just wouldn't be easier
to walk away
at times i feel i'm the only one this is important to.
that if i did walk away
you'd make no effort to change it.
i can't do this by myself.
i need to know "we" are as important to you
as "we" are to me.
you need to make an effort too.
not only will my life change
but yours too…
and i wonder if you truly realize that.
you seem to look at this as a one way street
when in fact it is the highway of life.

I find it very difficult to deal with issues with you
with your inability to discuss things rationally.

You seem to forget that things affect us both…
not only you.
That some things are out of our control
and that my job will always come first
as long as there is no long term commitment between us…
which
can either be considered my inability to make a move without marriage
or your inability to commit to marriage…
it depends upon which side of the fence you are on.
But it's a real problem when you literally cannot discuss things
and end a conversation without anything being resolved.
With two thousand miles between us
that reaction leads to major frustration…
for both of us.
I cannot survive in a relationship that does not allow discussion…
where situations are met with anger and defensiveness.
If we cannot discuss this we will have no where to go.

how are we to go on
when i feel that I am unable to voice my thoughts and feelings
without encountering your anger and defensiveness
if I am not allowed to air my beliefs
and you do not have the ability to even consider a thought
that is different than your own
than we have no future.
The world is larger than your view of it!
If life is to be lived solely on your terms…
centered on your selfish needs…
then there is no where for us to go together.

Chapter 9

Welcome to my Halloween nightmare. It's easy to say you know that something is ending, that this relationship is not really healthy for you, that you will survive when the time comes.

You're just never ready for the time to come.

All the months of trying-of being so close to the dream. I've learned one thing...to read what you write. Throughout the relationship I've written my poems of love and frustration...then tucked them away and never read them again...til it was all over.

The writing was on the wall...my own writing...if I'd only read it.

i knew that it was ending
i just wasn't sure when or how
well tonight was the night
and it was over the phone.
i had hoped that we would be together
and be able to discuss it as two adults
but i should have known that you would take the easy way out.
from your point of view
you can't take the two months of separation
which you've already endured.
and the reason for my canceling my visit last month
and that i canceled this month's visit was because of security reasons.
you now need to visit your ailing mother
which is totally valid.
i tell you that i will be down
as soon as you get back home.
you tell me to forget it
i say…oh i'm that easy to forget
you say you can't do the two months…
i say you just have
i say just go and get laid and get it over with
you say…oh…like there's someone to screw here
you say to just forget the whole thing
i say oh…we're just never going to see each other again
you say…no…call and come down sometime when you get a chance
i say no…i'll travel elsewhere
screw you…
end of relationship.

i hurt
but i don't cry
i'm angry…
that you couldn't look me in the eye…
that you took the easy way out.
i'm disappointed in myself
that i find satisfaction in the fact
that i am the best you ever had…
and that you will never find that again…
but that you are just a man…
no more or less
than i have known before…
i find peace in that…
and that makes me sad

so it's over
you are no more in my life.
how do i deal with that?
i love you…in spite of myself.
i have given my all to this…
believed in this…
in us.
and now it's over.
i can kid myself
and console myself
with thinking that you are shallow…
that you cannot see beyond the small island world
that you limit yourself to…
your self-proclaimed selfishness…
i thought i could accept it…
but even knowing what i know of you
i still love you
i cannot turn off the feelings…
eventually i will put the feelings away…
have fond memories of a wonderful love affair…
go on with my life

i sit and write
and listen to the wind chimes
that you gave me
they evoke memories
of happier times.
of day and nights filled with love
as the chimes sang in the gentle island breeze.
where to now?
you have cast me out to sea…
i am now adrift.
which new shore will i wash up upon…
what is waiting for me
in the roll of the next wave.
no matter…
i am ready to swim in the ocean of life.

i am the captain of my ship.
you may have thrown me overboard
into the rolling sea
but make no mistake
that i will wash up on the shore
and find my way.

i will not be a castaway
but the captain of my soul
i will navigate my journey
by my heart's desire
and find my way
in these unknown seas.

my anger supercedes all rational thought
if i could cry it might help
but i find it difficult to shed tears
over a love affair that was nothing but shallow
once again my dreams of love
have led my heart astray
where can i find comfort?
believing that i am more than you
gives me nothing
knowing that i gave all and lost
leaves me no where
once again
i have only me

the end.
even tho you were miles away
i felt secure.
it was nice knowing i was loved.
but what kind of love was it
that could be tossed aside so easily?
i gave you my all
and even that was not enough.
i cannot feel that i am at fault…
but that you have thrown away a gift.
how i wish you could speak your thoughts
and reveal your soul.
but that will never be
as your soul is hidden
even to yourself

once again i find myself alone.
i should not feel a stranger to this place…
rather that i have come home.
but i return a different person than the me who left
i have journeyed thru emotions and love
and experiences that have made me grow and learn.
now i am home and must take time to settle in
and prepare for the next journey.

today i start a whole new life.
i will never know your reasons
for ending our relationship.
true to form you avoided confrontation or explanation.
you are determined to live by your rules only…
there is no room for the consideration of another.
i hope you can at least confront yourself
and be true to yourself
in what this all means to your life

I am angry…
and at the same time relieved.
I think we both knew it was ending…
it was just how and when.

My anger stems from your inability to discuss anything
and the ease with which you walk away.
I will never know if, for you, there was any meaning to our relationship.

I understand only what I perceive to be you…
A self-admitted selfish man
whose emotions are locked within,
whose narrow vision allows no new thoughts or ideas,
who professes happiness and the ideal life
while seeing only the negative.

I saw all of this in you
and had hoped I could show you the optimistic side of life.
Not to change you
but to enlarge your world.
You have chosen your way
which you have every right to
and which I must accept.

I hope you take the time to reflect on your life
before you seek another relationship.
For only by being at peace with yourself
will you ever be successful in love.

what now?
i go on with my life.
i am falling in love with my house…
walking thru its rooms…bonding.
i am getting into my yard…
and finding good in the physical activity.
my work has taken on the importance
that I left behind a year ago.
i am again finding joy in my family and friends.
i am finding pleasure in all the simple things of life…
enjoying the beauty of a fall day…
meals with friends…
my grandchildren.
in honesty…
i am probably happier
than i have been in the last year…
no more limbo…
i have again taken control of my life.

one year ago today
we met in a small island bar.
little did we know
that a casual vacation fling
would turn into a love affair.
what a time we've had,
with monthly visits
filled with love and laughter.
never could a dark cloud
cover our days.
but as I relentlessly pursued marriage
as the only alternative
you slowly backed away
til you were left in the corner of choice.
i think you knew long ago
that you would never marry
and waited for an opportune moment
to use as your escape.
i think I knew long ago
that this is what you would do
but could not face the truth.
you have rarely surprised me.

Today would have been our first anniversary.
I was to be there celebrating with you.
dinner and drinks.
sweet, sweet love.
But a week ago
you decided you couldn't take
the extended time apart.
And I haven't heard from you since.
Did you ever consider that the extended time
is now a lifetime?
I'm sure I am better off by your choice.

now that i am over my anger
of your insensitivity in our parting
i can realize it is for the best.
you would have sucked the life out of me.
islands are small enough
but you have made your world even smaller
with your narrow views and lack of goals.
i see no quest for adventure
just the same ol', same ol' every day.
the façade you present to the world
fools no one but yourself.
whatever pain you hold deep within
has robbed you of the ability to love.
sad for me…
sadder for you.

i hesitate to write
knowing how you grasp the written word
only to throw it back
yet write i must
to gain closure for myself

did your heart flutter
at the sight of the envelope?
wasn't it grand to love and be loved
or were you only loved?
i have barely anything of you
while you have all of me

do you understand another person's needs?
that sometimes life situations step in
and you cannot always be first
that love is giving
not always receiving

just because you preface
a relationship
by saying you are selfish
does not give you the right
to not give back
that which you wish to receive
love is a two way street

treating someone good
is more than dinner

and being polite
it is listening with an open mind
caring about another person's needs
no one expects another to change
but ideas need to be shared
there is more than one way
to get to the same destination

why was it only my responsibility
to see you
you could have made the effort
to come here
you had your life to live
just as i had mine
but it was still up to me

what kind of love is yours
that can be tossed aside with a word?
what kind of man are you
that cannot face the parting?
anything goes without confrontation
i deserved better than this

when will you see
that the world is not as narrow
as you make it?
when will you ever hear
another's thoughts
that do not follow yours?

island life is small enough
but you have made yours even narrower
with the same ol' same ol' every day
and no room to vary
there is no adventure left in you

and as much as you say
life is good
you are a pessimist
with the glass half empty

i do not know
why you live on the island
but i believe
it allows you
to be a person
you could not be
in mainstream society

i feel
you have hidden pain
deep inside
and that is what
motivates you
remember
you can fool the world
but not yourself
take time to listen to you

i see no joy in you
just because the sun shines every day
and you admit only to highs
does not mean that life is good
and that you are happy
you put on your façade for the world
but fool only yourself

in reality
you would have sucked the life out of me
with your negative attitude
and lack of wonder

you are needy
and i could fulfill those needs
but i too need to be sustained

i will never understand
the why of it all
the ending with no explanation
does your heart hurt just a little?
What do you do with the void?
or has it been filled
with meaningless sex

i gave you my all
i never wavered
i am the best you ever had
never to be found again
while i have met you before
and will meet you again

i will remember the good times
there were many
it's sad that now you will
only hold a place in my heart
when there could have been so much more

i will not forgive
that you could not face me like a man
that you took from me
the opportunity to know
that i was walking the beach for the last time
feeling the island sun
and hearing the breath of the ocean
i needed to say good-bye to the island

i also needed

to say good-bye to you
to know
that it was the last time
i would touch you, kiss you
make love to you
there was no ending
and for that
i will not forgive you

i tell myself
that i will return someday
just to give myself closure
with the island
it may or may not come true
but i know the choice is mine

for now my life here is good
as you were never part
of my world here
nothing has really changed
i have taken time to reassess my life
and make new goals
there will be other warm climes
to comfort me

as much as i wish
it all could have worked out
i know that for me
this is best
i wish you well
and i wish you peace

i loved you
as i have not loved
in years

i still love you
and yet believe
that given time
and effort
on both our parts
it all could have been
more than a memory

EPILOGUE

I still glance at your picture occasionally
And my thoughts of you are sweet.
I'm planning a trip back to the island
Where I'll say my last goodbyes
Then, for me, this journey will be complete.
We all have our paths to follow…
Along the way we may find love
And journey together.
We all have choices.